The Grateful Gra

Author: Tam McIntyre

ISBN: 979-8-9850275-0-1

For My Dear Husband Hafid, My Son Amir, and My daughters Amadi, Amaya, and Alani. Also a special thanks to my Mother and my siblings. Thanks for all of your love and support. I am very grateful to share my life with all of you.

Mommy Hopper is going out to get some food. Gregory the grasshopper wants to go out with her, but she does not think it is safe. Gregory is not happy. He wants to make new friends, but he has not met anyone since they got here.

Mommy does not change her mind. "Gregory, you are too small to go outside. They may hurt you out there. Once you are big enough, you can go outside any time you want," she promises. "Ok." He mumbles.

Once she leaves, Greg feels sad and lonely. Then someone knocks on the door. Who could it be? It is an insect that looks just like Gregory. He is just brown and little bigger. "Hi, I am Larry the locust," said the locust.

"Do you want to come outside?" Larry asks Gregory.
Gregory frowns. He remembers what Mommy Hopper said.
She thinks he is still too small.
He does not feel small at all. "Do I really look small?
Mommy Hopper thinks I'm still too small to go outside,"
Gregory says. "I think you are just fine.
Let us go play before she returns," Larry replies

Gregory decides that it is a great idea and goes outside with Larry. Larry shows Gregory how to jump. Larry can jump easily from leaf to leaf. Gregory has to jump harder to get anywhere. He is very small. Larry and Gregory are having fun.

The fun suddenly ends when a huge spider appears.
Gregory is very afraid. He tries to catch up with Larry,
but he is too slow. He does not want to be left behind.
The spider runs after them.
He shoots webs until one of them hits Gregory's foot.
Larry is running in front and does not see the spider.
He did not know that Gregory was in trouble and he
leaves him behind.

More webs hit Gregory and trap him under a very tall tree. Gregory cannot untangle himself.

As the spider prepares to eat Gregory, suddenly Benny the Blackbird spots the spider and swoops in to capture him.

Gregory tries to wiggle out of the webs, but they are too tight. He calls for help, but no one answers. He continues to wiggle, but it does not work. A trail of ants march towards the webs. Gregory screams, but they don't hear him. He tries again to wiggle free.

Greg remembers what Mommy Hopper always says: "Asking for help is a strength, not a weakness". "Please help me!" he cries with all his might. An ant turns and see him there. "Someone needs help," he announces to the others. They set to work and remove the webs.

Gregory is free. He is very grateful that the ants helped him. "Thank you all so much, you saved my life", Gregory told the ants. "No worries friend, we were happy to help you", said Anthony the Ant. The ants continue on their way. Gregory joins the ants and marches in one line with them. He becomes friends with Anthony.

Gregory sees a butterfly on his way. He has
never seen a real butterfly before.
He has only heard about them and
their splendid colors. He is very happy to
see a real one. He leaves the ants.
As Gregory gets closer to the butterfly,

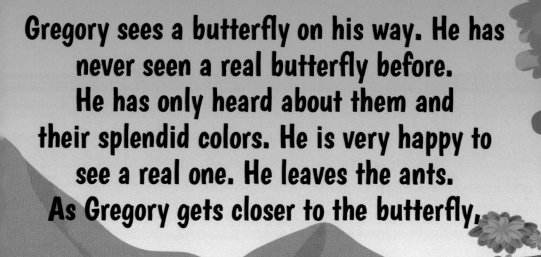

she notices him and says, "Hi, I am Betty the Butterfly.
What is your name?"
He is surprised that she is so pretty and nice to him.

"I am Gregory the Grasshopper.
I am new here," he tells her.
"You have the most beautiful wings."
"Thank you. Now Ri wants to meet you.
Sorry," says Betty. Then Betty pushes
Gregory off the branch.
He falls to the ground in front of
a smiling snake.

"Hi. I am Ri the Rattlesnake and I am going to eat you," Ri says. Gregory is scared. He does not want to be eaten. Ri smiles greedily and moves towards Gregory. Gregory shuts his eyes and thinks of Mommy Hopper. She will be so sad. She was right. He was too small to go outside. She only wanted to keep him safe.

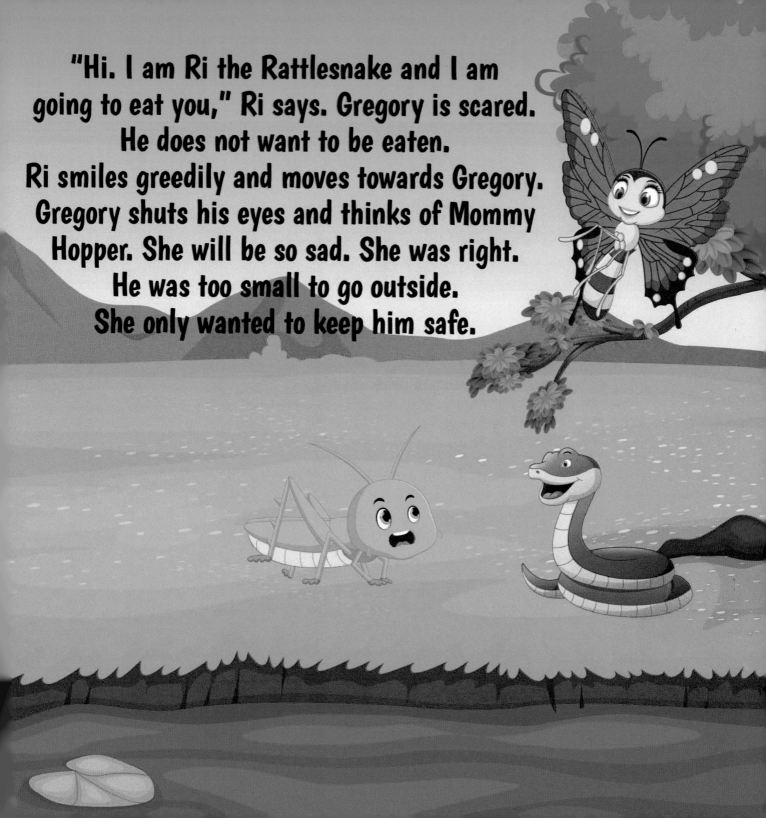

"Hop on!" he hears someone shout
and he opens his eyes.
It's Larry the locust!
Gregory hops on Larry's back and they
hop away before Ri can stop them.
Ri runs after them angrily, but he cannot
keep up. Luckily for them,

Larry is really fast, and they escape the snake.
Gregory is very grateful to see Larry again.

Suddenly, Benny the Blackbird reappears.
He grabs Gregory quickly and flies away.
Larry is shocked and afraid.

Benny lands in the grass and prepares
to eat Gregory when suddenly,
Oscar the Orange Tabby pounces
toward Benny from a nearby bush.
Benny shrieks loudly and quickly
takes flight!

"I am Gregory the Grasshopper. I need your help.
I need to go home," he tells the cat.
"I am Oscar the Orange Tabby. I will help you,"
the cat replies. "But first...
let's play," the cat said with a sly smile.
The cat begins to play very, very, roughly with Gregory.
Gregory does not like it at all.
"Please stop, you are hurting me," said Gregory.

"Oscar! Come here boy! What do you have there?"
said the boy. The boy steps over to Oscar
and sees the grasshopper under his paw.
"Wow! A real grasshopper!" exclaimed the boy.
"Let's keep him!"

Gregory remembers how Larry taught him to jump really high. At that moment, Gregory jumped as high as he possibly could, landing in a nearby bush.

Since the bush is almost the same color as
Gregory, he is hidden safely for now.
He decides to stay there. He does not know what to do.
He feels sad, lonely, and scared. Gregory begins to cry.

Suddenly, Gregory spotted a trail of ants walking
toward him. He remembers them.
They saved him from the spider web.
"Hey Anthony! It's me, Gregory! Boy, am
I glad to see you!! I want to go home,
but I don't know the way," he tells Anthony.
"I will help you," promised Anthony. Gregory joins
them once again.
He was very grateful to be back with the ants.

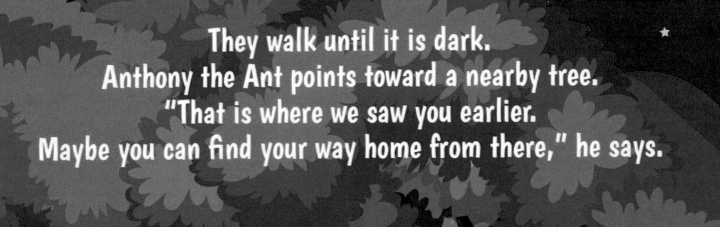

They walk until it is dark.
Anthony the Ant points toward a nearby tree.
"That is where we saw you earlier.
Maybe you can find your way home from there," he says.

Gregory thanks him and hops to
the tree. He is afraid that the snake
or the bird or even the
butterfly will find him.
Greg is afraid and alone again.

At that moment, Gregory hears a familiar voice.
It is Larry!! "Gregory!" Larry cries. "I have been
looking everywhere for you. We have
to go home now. Mommy Hopper is worried."
Gregory hops onto his back and together,
they return home. Gregory is very grateful
that Larry has come to save him again..

Mommy Hopper is outside. She looks very worried. "Where have you been? I have been worried sick about you!" said Mommy Hopper. "I went outside to play, I am sorry," he apologizes. "How did you find your way home in the dark?"she asks. "I asked for help like you always told me," said Gregory. "I met a spider, some ants, a butterfly, a snake, a blackbird, a cat, a boy, and a locust! Some of them were good and some of them were bad, but I learned that you cannot trust everyone, even those who look beautiful and smile at you. But there are some friends who will be true and kind. I also learned that there is danger all around. It can be very unsafe for a small hopper like me, especially when I am alone. Now I know that you ALWAYS knew what was best for me and I will never forget that. I will always listen to you and remember the things that you teach me. I am very grateful to have a Mommy like you! I love you Mommy Hopper!"

Gregory is very grateful to be back home safely. He is also glad to have some new friends.

Made in United States
Orlando, FL
02 September 2022

21906939R00018